PATIENCE'S FAITH

THE AMISH SISTERS

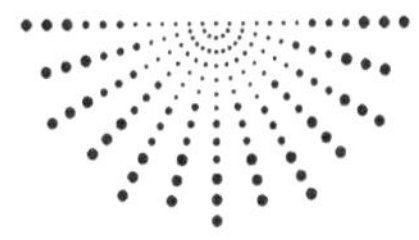

SARAH MILLER

SWEETBOOKHUB.COM

Welcome to my new book. It is one of three books about three Amish Sisters. Each book can be read alone but I'm sure you will love all of them.

Eliza's Faith

Patience's Faith

Annie's Faith

If you love Amish romance join my Newsletter. I will let you know as soon as my new books are available. You will also get occasional exclusive free books. You can join here

Blessings,

Sarah Miller

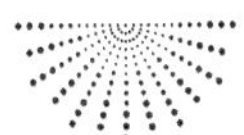

CHAPTER ONE

Faith's Creek, Pennsylvania.

To be the youngest of three sisters is always hard. You are always watching your older sisters grow and spread their wings. You see them find their place in the world, while you are still looking for yours. You see them happy when your own dreams go unfulfilled. Such was the lot for Patience Graber who, at nineteen years old, had watched her eldest sister Annie realize her ambition to become a schoolteacher and her middle sister Eliza marry the man she loved. Now it was Patience who had to live up to her name. She was a romantic and dreamed of love. Her dreams of finding a husband were still unfulfilled and though she knew it was wrong to wish the time would come... she couldn't help herself.

"You're still young, Patience, you only had your rumspringa a season ago. Give it time, have patience, Patience," her mamm, Barbara Graber would reply when Patience made her feelings known.

But still, the thought remained, and as time went by, she longed to find a husband and settle down. In that regard, she took after her sister Eliza, and though she knew that jealousy was a terrible sin, she could not help but feel it in her heart whenever her sister and her handsome husband, Matthew, came to visit.

They lived in a farmhouse not far away across the cornfields, and Patience would often go and visit them, helping her sister with the animals or sharing a simple meal with them. But it always pained her to see how happy Eliza was in her new life. Though she was happy for her sister, she yearned of sharing that happiness by finding a romance of her own. Faith's Creek had been her home all her life. She loved its rolling landscape, pretty houses, and simple way of life; yet, she could not help but wonder if she would ever find a husband there.

The men of Faith's Creek were good men and though she had known many of them all her life, there was not one among them that attracted her. It was as though over-familiarity and the bonds of friendship prevented any romantic feelings from emerging, a fact which made Patience ever more impatient with her search.

"What about James Kauffman? He's a nice boy, he always says 'hello' when I pass by the farm if he's working in the fields. Perhaps I could introduce the two of you?" Barbara said one afternoon.

Patience bit back a sigh, she knew her *mamm* was trying to help and shook her head. "He's nice, but I've known him since I was knee-high. I want to meet someone new, someone I don't know yet," she replied, sighing, as she sat at the table. Her *mamm* was elbows deep in flour, for it was the morning of baking day, the kitchen already smelled of cinnamon and cloves, sweet and fragrant.

"Didn't you have enough of meeting new men during your rumspringa?" Barbara asked.

Patience smiled. "I don't want a man from just anywhere *Mamm*, he has to share our values, like

Matthew does. Eliza's so happy, I just want that, too," she replied, as her eldest sister Annie came clattering down the stairs.

"Don't forget those work books there, Annie," Barbara said, pointing to a pile of books on the table.

"Oh, thank you, *Mamm*, I'd forget my head if it weren't screwed on. What a rush," she said, snatching up the books and kissing their *mamm* goodbye.

"Will you be back for dinner at noon?" Barbara called out, but Annie was gone, the porch door banging behind her.

"Now there's a girl who doesn't have time for a husband," Barbara said, and Patience smiled.

"I know not everyone wants to get married, but I do. Annie made up her mind a long time ago to be a schoolteacher, it's all she's ever wanted to do. But all I've ever wanted is to find a husband, and I can't even do that," she said, sighing and putting her head into her hands.

"Oh, Patience, enough of this. Sometimes, when I've lost something, I search and search for it and can't find it. But when I stop looking, it turns up, just like that. Maybe you should look a little less hard and not expect so much," Barbara replied with a chuckle.

"Do you need any help this morning or can I walk over to Eliza's?" Patience asked, and her *mamm* laughed.

"You've got a face that would turn milk today, Patience, and I don't think it'll be any help in raising bread and cakes. Go over to see your sister, tell her I said she has to cheer you up. Go on now," she said.

Patience kissed her mother's smooth cheek and straightened her kapp before stepping out into the sunshine. It was late July, the cornfields swaying gently in the breeze, a patchwork of golden colors spread out before her. The lane toward Faith's Creek wound its way across the fields, and she smiled at the sound of birds singing in the trees above.

"Off out already, Patience? Your sister was in such a rush she didn't even see me," her *daed*, Samuel called out.

He was weeding in the vegetable patch, his large straw hat all that was visible above the bean stalks growing up the trellis which ran the length of the patch.

"I'm going to see Eliza, *Mamm* said I could," Patience called out, and Samuel waved his hand.

"Say 'hello' to your sister from me, and tell Matthew I've got those seeds he wanted, though he'll have to be quick if he wants to plant them," he called back.

Patience set out to walk to the home of Eliza and Matthew. It was only a mile away, and as she walked, she greeted their friends and neighbors along the way. Her sister was outside feeding the chickens when Patience arrived, and she waved to her, beckoning her through the gate and hurrying to embrace her.

"This is a nice surprise, I thought you'd be helping *Mamm* with the baking," Eliza said.

She was a pretty woman, and Patience had always envied her looks. She considered herself to be somewhat plain, though in truth she was just as pretty as her sister, with blonde hair and blue eyes. Eliza's hair being darker; of course, you could hardly tell from the few strands that escaped her kapp.

"She said I was too miserable to help her bake, that nothing would rise if I stayed around," Patience replied, causing her sister to laugh.

"Well, don't bring that sour face in here, I don't want my milk turning. Come on in, I'll make us some coffee and you can tell me what's wrong. I'm sure it's not that bad." Eliza ushered Patience up the steps onto the porch.

Matthew had only just finished building the house and everything was brand new. It was a cozy place, the door opening into a parlor with a range and chairs, a sideboard and table, with a door leading into the kitchen beyond. Eliza had made cross-stitch pictures for the walls and woven a rug for the floor. Patience loved visiting her sister, even if in her company she was reminded of what she did not yet possess.

"Oh, *Daed* says that the seeds Matthew wants are ready, though you need to plant them quick," Patience said, settling herself down in her favorite chair by the stove.

"He's over at Bishop Beiler's house at the moment fixing the fence, we can tell him when he gets back.

Now, what's the matter? I can see there's something not right," Eliza said, putting on a kettle to boil and coming to sit opposite Patience, who sighed.

"Why don't prayers get answered?" she asked.

Eliza looked at her in surprise. "What a thing to say, Patience, you know they do, but you also know that *Gott* doesn't just grant us every demand we make," Eliza replied, tutting at Patience, who shook her head.

"But all I've prayed for is happiness, Eliza. I've prayed for a husband and my prayers haven't been answered," Patience replied, folding her arms in a sulk.

Ever since she had seen Eliza courting Matthew, her one prayer, every night before bed, as she kneeled in her bedroom, was that *Gott* would send her a husband. She thought she could only be happy again if that one prayer was answered and the more she prayed, the further away she felt from that prayer being answered.

"Oh, Patience, happiness isn't dependent on a man, it's not dependent on anyone or anything but *Gott*. It's *Gott* that gives us happiness, everything else is just grass, burned up in the furnace, fleeting moments. Don't be fooled by the world into thinking you need a husband to be happy," Eliza replied, reaching out and taking Patience by the hand.

"That's easy for you to say. You've got everything you ever wanted. A husband, a home, a life together. That's all I want, too." Patience said.

Eliza smiled. "Don't set your standards on others, Patience. We all have things we want, things we don't have, dreams unfulfilled. I'll say it again, if you base your happiness on finding a husband, and that alone, then it's no happiness at all. I've told you this before, we all have. Look at Annie, isn't she happy? She's not got a husband, but she's got something precious to her. Where your treasure is, there your heart is, too, that's what the scriptures say. You need to find what really gives you joy. It doesn't have to be a man," Eliza said, as the kettle boiled on the stove.

As Eliza made the drinks, Patience thought about what her sister had said. She had said it before, of course, for this was not the first time that Patience had come to her in distress. But as the months went by, Patience was growing ever more despondent at the prospect of finding the man she dreamed of. She was not willing to settle for just anyone, but it seemed that everyone in Faith's Creek was taken, the hope of finding the right man seemed to be growing fainter day by day.

"But what else is there?" Patience asked.

Eliza tutted. "You could give more service to the church, you could start your own little business or a small holding, you could even help Annie at the schoolhouse. You have too much time on your hands, Patience," Eliza said, just as footsteps on the porch announced the arrival of Matthew.

Patience had always liked him, there was something about his smile that drew her to him, and now he greeted her warmly, sitting down heavily in one of the chairs, as Eliza poured out the coffee.

"Did you get the fence fixed?" she asked.

Matthew nodded. "Those winds we had last week had clean blown it down. It didn't take long to fix it, but Bishop Beiler was pleased. Sarah says she'll bake us a cake to thank us," he said.

Eliza smiled. "We don't need thanking. Bishop Beiler's done more than enough for us," Eliza said, sitting down next to Matthew, and taking a sip of her drink.

"He was saying that the Smithson place is let," Matthew said.

Eliza's eyes widened. "That old place up on the hill over there?" she exclaimed, gesturing behind her.

Matthew nodded.

Abraham Smithson had been an eccentric, and when he died, his family had wanted nothing to do with Faith's Creek or their strange ways. The house had lain empty for years and was so run down it seemed impossible that anyone would wish to rent it.

"A man named Noah King from Ohio, a widower, and his nephew Caleb. They moved in two days ago. I thought I saw some lights up there the other night, but I assumed it was just kids messing around. Still, they're our neighbors and we'd best make them welcome," Matthew said.

Eliza nodded. "We should invite them for dinner, Matthew, make them feel welcome. You'll come, too, won't you Patience?" she asked.

Patience nodded. "I wonder what they're like," she said, her imagination running away with her.

She could not remember the last time anyone had come to live in Faith's Creek, and she was curious to meet these newcomers, imagining the possibility of romance.

"No, Patience, don't get carried away. For all you know the nephew might bring a bride with him, or be betrothed. They might not even be of our community," Eliza replied.

Patience's face fell. *How could her sister read her thoughts so easily?*

"Oh, they're Amish, all right, no doubting that. Bishop Beiler told me," Matthew said, smiling at Patience, who felt her heart begin to race.

"When will you invite them?" she asked, and Eliza laughed.

"Just as soon as they've settled in. I'll walk up there tomorrow and speak to them. It'll be interesting to see the old place. Do you remember when we used to play in the woods up there as *kinner*? Mr. Smithson was always so kind, he didn't mind us running over his vegetable patch or swinging in the trees in his orchard," she said, smiling and shaking her head.

But Patience was not thinking about the past, only the present and she leaped up from her chair, excusing herself on a most important errand.

"But you only just arrived," Eliza said, as she and Matthew looked at Patience curiously.

"Oh, I just remembered I need to go and... speak to... Mr. Jacobs about the... something for *mamm*," she said, and before Eliza could reply, Patience had rushed out of the house.

She wanted to catch a glimpse of their new neighbors, curious as to what they were like. Her heart racing fast, she set off along the lane which led back toward her parent's house, veering off at the fork which led up to Abraham Smithson's house, the house now let to the newcomers. She could pretend she was taking the long way home, ambling as she went until she came in sight of the house, which lay up a short track, surrounded by a large garden and trees.

She and Eliza used to play there when they were little and now Patience recalled the kindly Mr.

Smithson, who tolerated the two little Graber girls and was always happy to let them pick his strawberries or taken a pinny full of apples home to their *mamm*. As she passed the house, Patience could see a young man working in the garden. He was only a year or two older than her, tall and blond, with a muscular build and an angular face.

Patience was immediately taken by him, and she hid behind a tree, just off the lane, watching him curiously. He was working hard, the sweat glistening on his brow, and she imagined their introduction, the words they would speak, her heart racing with excitement. Just then, a shout from inside the house brought the man inside, downing his tools and mopping his brow. Patience was disappointed, but in that brief glimpse, she was certain she had seen the possibility of all her dreams.

"You look much more cheerful now," her *mamm* said, as Patience arrived home for dinner that afternoon, "did your sister make things better?"

"Oh, she helped a lot," Patience said, helping herself to a freshly baked cinnamon bun, and smiling, "I think things might be looking up."

"I can't believe they let the Smithson place. It's a wreck," Samuel said, shaking his head, as he sat down at the breakfast table the next morning.

"They're doing a lot to it, already," Patience said, and her *mamm* and *daed* looked up with puzzled expressions on their faces.

"How do you know that?" Barbara asked.

Patience felt heat hit her cheeks, why did she have to blush? "Oh, Eliza said, well, Matthew told us, but they're going to invite them over for dinner, the new tenants, that is. Eliza says I can come, too, and help make them welcome," Patience said.

Barbara chuckled. "This wouldn't happen to have anything to do with a young nephew, now, would it?"

Patience blushed even deeper. "*Mamm!* But there's never anyone new in this place, I want to meet new people."

Samuel was also amused and raised his eyebrows as he fought down his own laughter. "I'm sure your sister can be trusted to look after you. She always had a kind heart. It's just like Eliza to invite the new neighbors over for dinner."

Barbara took a sip of her coffee and shared a look with her husband before bringing her eyes back to her daughter. "Now, Patience, I need you to come to the market with me this morning. I can't carry everything by myself. Your *daed's* going to take us in the buggy. Get yourself ready now," Barbara said, just as Annie clattered down the stairs.

"You need a lesson in punctuality." Samuel chuckled again, as Annie grabbed a cinnamon bun from the table and hurried to the door.

"It isn't my fault the rooster won't crow anymore, I slept right through. I've been so busy with preparations for the auction, I've not been going to bed until past midnight," Annie called back, as the door banged on its hinges.

"Oh, she works so hard. She loves that school. I do hope the fundraising auction goes well. Come on then, Patience, get yourself ready." Barbara was already clearing the table.

Soon they had donned their capes and the two of them stepped out into the morning sunshine.

Patience enjoyed shopping with her *mamm* at the market on a Thursday morning. It was a day when the entire community of Faith's Creek gathered together, the stalls laden with all manner of good things to eat, plants, crafts, and other goods for sale. They had a list of things to buy and Barbara was soon talking to her friends and acquaintances, while Patience explored the stalls and breathed in the atmosphere of the market. It seemed that new sights awaited everywhere she looked.

"Is that gooseberry jam, Mr. Coblentz?" she asked, picking up a jar and peering at the contents.

"Oh, did I forget to label that one? Let me see, now. I think it's damson. That's right, I had a glut of them off the tree last November and I remember boiling them up for the jam. It's been in the cupboard all these months, but it'll taste good now. You can have it for half the price, seeing as I'm not certain what's in there," he said, smiling, as Patience rummaged in her pocket.

She had always liked talking to Mr. Coblentz, who seemed able to make even the most meager of harvests into something interesting.

"Do you have any pickles? My *daed* loves those pickled onions you make," she asked, peering over the stall in search of the elusive jar.

"I just sold the last one, to those newcomers from Ohio. But you can have some beets, just jarred them last week," he said.

Patience shook her head. "Beetroot brings him out in a rash, don't you remember the cookout two summers ago? He turned the same color when Mrs. Wagler served him her apple surprise cake. The surprise was, she put beetroot in it, like a carrot cake. I don't think my *daed* appreciated it," Patience replied, as Mr. Coblentz laughed.

"You best stick to the jam, then Patience, I've not seen anyone find anything wrong with that. Not so far, at least. Good day to you," he said, turning to serve another customer.

Patience looked around for her *mamm*, spotting her talking to Sarah Beiler by Katy Zook's cake stall. Patience hurried through the crowd, but her foot caught on a dropped box and she stumbled, dropping the jar of jam clean out of her hands. It smashed on the floor, splattering her with jam, the smell confirmed it was indeed damson.

"Oh, butter fingers," she exclaimed, brushing the mess off her skirt, which only seemed to stain it further.

"Here, let me help you," a voice above her said, and she looked up to find a tall, slender man with graying hair and a matching beard.

He smiled at her, his soft green eyes twinkling, as he kneeled down to pick up the pieces.

"Thank you," she exclaimed, "I'm not normally this clumsy. I tripped on something and then... no jam for me."

"These things can be cleaned up and we can all be a little clumsy at times. The main thing is that you are unhurt... there, I think that's the last of the glass," he said.

Patience was overwhelmed with his kindness. "*Denke*," she said, as he helped her to her feet. Before she said anymore he tipped his hat, and ambled off into the crowd.

She watched him for a moment, wondering who he was. She had not seen him before, though he seemed to remind her of someone, his kindness a small compensation for the loss of the jam.

"Are you all right, Patience?" Barbara asked, hurrying over to her.

"I'm fine, it's just my dress, that's all," she said

"It's easily washed. Come along, your *daed* doesn't like to be kept waiting."

Patience followed her mamm, occasionally searching the crowd for the man who had helped her. For some reason, she wanted to thank him once more.

CHAPTER THREE

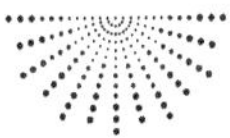

As they rode home in the buggy, Patience thought about her encounter with the stranger in the market. She was curious to know who he was. He had certainly been kind to her and she hoped to have the chance to thank him once again.

"Oh, look, there's Eliza, she must be going to the house," Barbara said, pointing along the lane.

Patience could see her sister up ahead, the three of them hailing her as they passed.

"Climb in," Samuel said, as he reined the horse to a halt and held out his hand to Eliza, who climbed up next to Patience.

"What happened to you? Is that blood?" Eliza exclaimed, looking at Patience's dress.

Patience laughed. "*Nee*, it's the last pot of damson jam left in Faith's Creek. Unfortunately, you won't be tasting it," she said.

Eliza laughed. "You always were clumsy," she said, tutting, and shaking her head.

"No, I wasn't!" Patience folded her arms and looked sulkily at her sister. She hated it when Eliza pointed out her faults, but Eliza only smiled at her.

"Cheer up, I've got some news for you. I've visited our new neighbors, Mr. King, and his nephew, and I've invited them for dinner. They were only too happy to accept. Now, are you going to sulk over that?" Eliza asked.

Patience's eyes brightened. "Did you tell them I'd be there, too?" she asked, and Eliza nodded.

"I said my sister would be there, and that she was looking forward to meeting them, too," Eliza replied.

Patience knew it was silly but she was sure that her heart skipped a beat at the excitement to come. "When?" she asked.

Eliza glanced at their *mamm* and *daed*. "Tonight. There's no time like the present and I wanted to make them feel welcome. They've nothing in and it seemed the least I could do to make them a nice dinner," Eliza replied.

"Oh, how exciting. I can go, can't I, *Mamm*? Eliza promised and *Daed* said..." Patience began, her parents both started laughing.

"You leave me out of this, Patience," Samuel said, as they pulled up outside the house.

"I'm not one to break promises, you know that. You can go, but be sure to be a help to your sister and don't make a nuisance of yourself. Speak when you're spoken to and listen before you speak," Barbara replied, but Patience was not listening, for she was far too excited at the prospect of the evening, imagining what it would be like to have dinner with Caleb and his uncle.

It was as though she had already imbued him with all the qualities she desired in a husband. She was so excited to meet him and discover if what she thought to be true, really was.

"Well, come for six o'clock, Matthew can walk you

home, or bring you in the buggy," Eliza said, as she bid her parents and Patience goodbye.

It was still only late in the morning and Patience could not imagine waiting so long, her excitement was building by the moment.

"I'll be there," she said, waving to Eliza, before hurrying off inside, eager to prepare herself for what was to come.

"I don't think so, Patience. What will your *daed* say when he sees that?" her *mamm* said, as Patience emerged from the bathroom with her hair plaited in two tails and ribbons hanging down.

"No one will see it... *Daed* won't even see it... I'll be wearing my kapp," she complained, and her mamm frowned.

"Take out the ribbons and put it up, properly, Patience, or shall I do it for you?" Barbara replied.

With a sigh Patience returned to her bedroom and

arranged her hair neatly under her kapp, glancing at herself in the mirror as she did so.

She sighed, imagining herself to be terribly plain, although her sisters and *Mamm* always told her she was pretty, Patience was not convinced, telling herself that even if Caleb noticed her he would not wish for anything more than friendship.

"Is that better?" she asked when she stepped back out onto the landing.

Barbara nodded. "Much better. Now, off you go, your sister is expecting you," she said, as the two of them made their way downstairs.

"Enjoy your evening and remind Matthew to come and pick those seeds up," her *daed* called out after her.

It was nearly six o'clock, and Patience hurried along the lane, taking a shortcut across the fields. She was rehearsing what she might say, hoping that she would not make a fool of herself or say anything to embarrass herself. Eliza was feeding the chickens in the garden and she waved to Patience, who looked around her expectantly, surprised to find her sister outside.

"Are they not here yet?" she asked.

Eliza shook her head. "I told them to come at half-past. Come along inside, you can help me peel the last of the potatoes."

With only the slightest disappointment, Patience followed her inside.

Matthew was sitting by the stove and he rose to greet her, smiling, as she rolled her sleeves up.

"Point me to them," she said, fighting down her disappointment that their guests had not yet arrived.

The smell of something delicious was coming from the oven and Eliza pointed to a pile of potatoes on the side, glancing at the clock, which now showed the quarter past.

"Get them peeled and we'll have them on to boil before they arrive," she said, handing Patience a potato peeler.

Soon, the potatoes were peeled and Patience was just putting the last of them into a pan of water when a knock came at the door.

"I'll get it," she said, eager to be the first to introduce herself formally to Caleb and his uncle.

Eliza nodded, the two sisters smoothing down their skirts, as Patience hurried to the door. Her heart was racing as she flung it open, about to greet the man she had already married in her heart. But it was not the tall, muscular blond young man she had seen from afar but instead the man from the market, the one who had assisted her following the accident with the jam.

"Good evening," he said.

Patience was quite lost for words.

CHAPTER FOUR

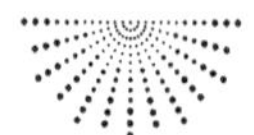

"Good evening, Mr. King," Eliza said, stepping past Patience, who was too surprised to speak, "Do come in, where are Patience's manners?"

"Oh, it's quite all right, Mrs. Lloyd, I think Patience is surprised to see me. We met earlier today. I'm Noah King, Patience, I should have introduced myself earlier on, my apologies," he said, holding out his hand to Patience, who by now had regained her composure.

"It's a pleasure to meet you, I... it was Mr. King who helped me when I dropped the jar of jam earlier," she said, blushing at the memory.

"Well, we owe Mr. King our thanks," Eliza said, closing the door behind him, as Patience turned with a disappointed look on her face.

"It's ever so kind of you to invite me," he said, as Matthew came to shake his hand.

"I'm only sorry that my nephew can't join us. He's feeling rather under the weather today. I think he's been working too hard out in the sun these past few days. You know how it is," Noah replied.

He had a pleasant voice, gentle and soothing. Patience liked him, but she was sad that the object of her interests had not been able to make the dinner that evening.

"Won't you sit down?" Eliza asked, pointing to the table, which was laid prettily with their best crockery and a vase of freshly cut flowers.

"I must say, the hospitality here in Pennsylvania is second to none," Noah said, taking up his napkin, and taking a deep breath, "The food smells delicious. I had Bishop Beiler and his wife round at the house earlier on. They brought a basket of fruit and a cake, it was so kind."

"We're a tight-knit community here in Faith's Creek. What was it like in Ohio?" Matthew asked as Eliza busied herself in the kitchen.

Patience was busy fetching and carrying the dishes through to the table.

"Ohio is Ohio, our last crop failed, that's what brought us here. We had no money left and I wasn't going to risk another unpredictable season. You've got good soil here, it's well known, and I knew this was the right place the first time I laid eyes on it. There's something about it, it's got a good feeling to it," Noah said, smiling at them.

"Well, we're glad you're here," Matthew replied, smiling back at Noah as he did so.

There was roast chicken for dinner, boiled potatoes, and vegetables fresh from the garden. Noah told them more about Ohio and his farm there, explaining that he had lost his wife to a fever some years previously.

"She was my rock, but *Gott* chose to take her, though I was blessed with Caleb. He lost his parents around the same time in a buggy accident, and the two of us shared our grief. I wouldn't know what to do without him," Noah said, shaking his head.

"It sounds like *Gott* gave you what you needed, just when you needed it," Eliza replied, as she began to clear the plates

"You're right about that, Mrs. Lloyd," Noah replied.

"It's Eliza, Mr. King, we don't need to stand on ceremony," she said, and Noah nodded.

"Then call me, Noah, and I hope that tonight marks the beginning of a friendship between our families," he said.

"You've still got the rest of them to meet, there's our *mamm*, Barbara, and our *daed*, Samuel. Our eldest sister is Annie, and she's the schoolmistress here in Faith's Creek. We're very proud of her, aren't we, Patience?" Eliza said.

Patience looked up. She had been lost in thought over Caleb, wondering if she would ever meet him and now, she stammered, caught out by her sister's question.

"Oh... yes, very," she said.

Eliza raised her eyebrows. "Stop your daydreaming, Patience, and help me to clear the table. We've still got dessert to have yet."

Patience dutifully rose to her feet.

It was apple cobbler for dessert, Eliza had just finished dishing up when a knock came at the door.

"Now who could this be?" Eliza said as Matthew went to open it.

Patience had two dishes in hand and was just emerging from the kitchen, as Matthew ushered in their latest guest. She almost dropped the two dishes in surprise, for it was Caleb who stood in the parlor, apologizing for his tardiness.

"I'm sorry, Mrs. Lloyd, I don't know what came over me. My head was aching, and I was so thirsty. I just had to lie down for a while. I hope you don't mind me appearing like this," he said, as Eliza emerged from the kitchen behind Patience.

"Mind? Of course, we don't mind. Come and sit yourself down, I'll give you a double helping of dessert to make up for missing the first course. Patience, will you bring another chair?" Eliza said

Patience nodded, setting down the dishes on the table and eyeing Caleb nervously.

He had an air of confidence about him, one which she found unsettling. Patience was naturally shy, unused to speaking in public or being the center of attention. Now, her well-rehearsed words were forgotten, and she sat nervously next to Eliza, listening as the conversation continued.

"We're going to plant tomatoes, too," Caleb was saying, "though I'm not sure we've chosen the variety yet, we want the best for the area."

"I can give you some help with that. I've been growing tomatoes in this soil since I was a boy," Matthew replied. "But you'll have to wait until next year, now. You're too late for tomatoes now,"

"Oh, I know that, Mr. Lloyd, but we're keen to make the land pay," Caleb said, tucking into his dessert with gusto.

"There's the orchard to clear up, too, it's so overgrown, but I'm sure there are all sorts of different fruit trees under the tangle of weeds and brambles," Noah said.

"We'll help you in any way we can," Matthew said.

Noah thanked him profusely. "To good neighbors," he said, raising his glass of water, and the others followed suit.

Patience had barely said a word, and she wondered if Caleb had even noticed her, for he had addressed not a single question to her. She felt deflated, though she knew her dreams had been foolish and fantastical. The thought that Caleb would immediately take a shine to her or speak of courting was quite ridiculous, though she could only admit it had been a pleasant one.

"Clear the table, Patience," Eliza said when dessert was over.

Patience nodded, rising from the table and taking Noah's dish from in front of him.

But her hands were trembling, as she glanced at Caleb, and she dropped the dish clean to the floor, where it smashed into a dozen shards, causing Eliza to shriek.

"I'm sorry," Patience cried, as Matthew hurried to get the broom.

"Oh, Patience, you must be more careful. Never mind, there's no harm done. What is it *Mamm* always says? Better a broken plate than a broken bone," Eliza said, as Matthew began to sweep up the shards of crockery.

"You've got a habit of letting things slip through your fingers, Patience," Noah said, smiling at her.

Patience turned red as a beet.

"Uncle Noah, that's not very polite, look at the poor girl, you've embarrassed her," Caleb said, smiling at Patience, who now blushed even further.

The broken crockery was soon swept away, and it seemed that the breaking of the dish was also the breaking of the ice. Caleb now took an interest in Patience, asking her a little about herself and talking animatedly about his hopes for the farmstead and the orchard.

"We've had a delightful evening, Eliza. The three of you must come up to us next time, bring your *mamm* and *daed*, your sister, too. I've a feeling we're all going to get on like family," Noah said when it came for them to wish their hosts goodnight.

"It's been our pleasure to have you here," Eliza replied, as the three of them stood on the porch and wished Noah and Caleb goodnight.

"Say," Caleb said, turning to Patience, "why don't you show me around a bit, tomorrow. I hear the walk by the creek is just lovely."

Patience felt her heart skip a beat, and she glanced at Eliza, who nodded.

"I'd love to, we can walk right along by the water's edge. It's lovely down there. We often walk there, don't we, Eliza?" Patience said, and Eliza nodded.

"I'm sure you'll show Caleb everything Faith's Creek offers. It's such a pretty place, and I'm sure you'll fit right in," Eliza said, as they wished their new friends goodnight.

But as they left, having agreed that Caleb would call for Patience at noon the next day, Patience could not help but notice the uncomfortable look that crossed Noah's face, it was as though he held some concern about Caleb's offer.

"Do you think *Mamm* will mind if I go to walk with

Caleb tomorrow?" Patience asked as Matthew prepared to walk her home.

"I don't think she could stand the disappointment in your voice or the month of moping if she refused. Besides, I don't mind walking behind you, though I'm sure his intentions are entirely honorable."

"*Denke*," Patience said as her mind wandered to the joys of the walk.

"Well, goodnight, Patience, and try not to drop anything else before bed tonight," Eliza said, kissing Patience on the cheek.

As Matthew walked her home that evening, full of praise for their new neighbors, Patience wondered what the next day would bring and why Noah had had such a strange expression on his face at the mention of her and Caleb stepping out together.

CHAPTER FIVE

If Patience's *mamm* had thought for a moment that she would prevent Patience and Caleb from stepping out on their walk together, then she was sorely mistaken. Patience had risen early the next morning, informing Barbara that Eliza would be acting as a chaperone and that she and Caleb would only be taking a walk by the creek.

"Well, just remember your modesty, Patience," Barbara said.

Patience smiled, kissing her on the cheek, before straightening her kapp and putting on her shawl.

"It's only a walk, *Mamm*," she said.

Barbara smiled. "And there was me thinking you'd been waiting for this moment for years, Patience. Go on, enjoy yourself."

Patience skipped out of the porch door and down the steps across the garden.

She almost collided with her *daed* as she did so, flushing with embarrassment as he looked her up and down.

"You are so grown up. Make sure Eliza is there at all times," he said, smiling at her.

She nodded, before running off into the lane and taking the shortcut across the cornfields, to find her sister waiting outside the house.

"Oh, there you are, Patience, it's nearly noon. He'll be here in a moment," Eliza said, glancing up the lane in the direction of the Smithson place.

Patience looked too, and she could see the figure of Caleb strolling toward them, a straw hat perched jauntily on his brow. He waved to them, ambling up and offering Patience his arm.

"What a beautiful day for a walk," he said, glancing up into the clear blue sky.

Patience felt her heart skip a beat, she took his arm, suddenly growing shy and wondering if the contact was too much, too soon.

"It's very kind of you to offer to take Patience out like this, Caleb," Eliza said, and Caleb smiled.

"It's her that's going to show me round, I'm looking forward to it," he said.

Patience smiled. "Me, too. Let's go this way first. There's a path here that leads down to the creek," she said, pointing off across the meadow, where the grass gave way to trees, the water flowing below.

Eliza followed a short distance behind, and Patience and Caleb walked arm in arm, talking of this and that until they came to the path at the water's edge. He stooped down and picked up a stone, skimming it across the surface of the water, until it splashed, causing a fish to jump. Patience admired his confidence, the way he spoke and acted. He was a perfect gentleman, and she knew that her *mamm* and *daed* need have no worries about his intentions. This was the moment she had been waiting for, the one she had dreamed of so often, and now it was coming true.

"So, you like Faith's Creek? Did you ever think of leaving?" he asked.

Patience shook her head. "I'd never leave Faith's Creek, it's my home, my family's here and my life's here. I know everyone and everyone knows me. I think you'll be very happy here," she replied.

"I think so, too, although I preferred life back in Ohio. Still, you've got to make the best of things haven't you?" he said, picking up another stone and skimming it across the water.

"Give it a chance, I think you'll come to like it. We have such a lovely community here and you'll fit right in. Just wait until you come to your first cookout, or one of the board games nights up in the barns, they're always so much fun," she said.

He laughed. "Well, if there's one thing I'm certain of, it's that I'm glad I met you. That's enough to make me not so sad about leaving Ohio behind," he said.

Patience felt her cheeks blush. No man had ever spoken to her like that before. It seemed an astonishing thing to say, given how little they knew of one another, but she was so caught up in the moment that she could only smile and nod.

"And I'm glad you're here, too. We get so few newcomers, it's so nice to meet someone new, and..." she began, her tongue about to slip.

She had been about to say how handsome he was, but embarrassment overcame her, and she grew shy, turning away from him, her blush deepening.

"Back in Ohio, I used to think I had it all, and it was my Uncle Noah who wanted to come out here, but Faith's Creek doesn't seem so bad after all. They certainly welcome newcomers," he said, raising his hand and brushing his fingers against her cheek.

Patience was shocked by the boldness of his move and a tingle ran down her spine, goosebumps rising on her arms. She had never known a man to behave in such a way before and she glanced over her shoulder. Eliza's eyes were wide with shock and she was shaking her head.

"Oh my," was all she could say, and he offered her his hand, indicating for them to continue along the path by the creek.

She was unsure whether to take it, but he seemed too charming, so confident and interested, that she had no wish to dissuade him. Glancing again at Eliza, Patience took Caleb by the hand and they walked on, the two of them talking happily together. Patience felt as she imagined every woman who had fallen in love would feel. It was a strange sensation, overwhelming, in fact, but she presumed that this was how it must feel. Surely, she reasoned, it was normal to experience such things and for a man to behave in such a manner.

The path now rose from the creek, returning through the trees and into the cornfields. They had come in a large loop and were now almost back at the fork in the lane which would be their natural parting place. Patience did not want the walk to end. She was filled with excitement at the prospect of all that was to come, and she was already thinking of seeing Caleb again. He was everything she had ever imagined a man to be, and her heart was racing as they came to say their goodbyes.

"I've really enjoyed our walk, Patience. It's been great to get to know you and see the neighborhood. Faith's Creek sure is a pretty place. Can I see you again soon?" he asked.

She nodded, almost too excited to reply. "I'd like that, there's an auction at the schoolhouse on Monday. My sister's organizing it, it's a fundraising effort, there's so much they need to buy. Maybe you'd like to come?" she asked.

Caleb nodded. "I'd like to if you'll be there," he said, and Patience blushed, twisting her hands together as she smiled at him.

"Then I'll be there. It's on Monday afternoon, at three o'clock. You can't miss the schoolhouse, it's right by Bishop Beiler's house, with the blue slats and the little bell," she said.

"I'll find it, no problem, and I'll be counting the hours until I see you again," he said, smiling at her, as he waved to Eliza and ambled off up the hill toward the Smithson place.

Patience was overwhelmed, her heart fluttering at the thought of seeing Caleb again. He was everything she had ever imagined, everything she had ever dreamed of, and it seemed he wanted to be with her as much as she wanted to be with him.

"Oh, Eliza, did you see him just now? Isn't he just

wonderful?" Patience said, running up to her sister and throwing her arms around her.

"Now, Patience, don't get carried away, and be grateful that *Mamm* and *Daed* didn't see the two of you together down by the creek. I must say, I nearly intervened," Eliza said.

Patience made a face at her. "Didn't you and Matthew ever have your moments when you were courting?" she asked.

Her sister smiled. "We had our moments, yes. But I've known Matthew since we were knee-high. You've known Caleb all of five minutes. I know you're excited, but don't get too caught up in him, you hear me?"

Patience only shook her head and smiled. "Can't you just be happy for me? He's perfect and I like him, isn't that enough?" Patience asked, still caught up in the thought of Caleb and his smile.

"I'm just warning you, Patience. He's a nice young man, and his uncle is most pleasant and affable, but don't get so caught up in your hopes that you forget to see where you're going. There's no rush in matters of the heart. You have to be certain," Eliza said, as they walked back along the lane.

But Patience had already made up her mind, and she knew that the days to come would be long and drawn out, as she waited to see Caleb again and discover what might be.

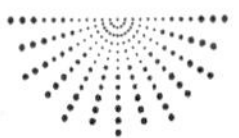

CHAPTER SIX

"Oh, no. You stop right there, young lady," Samuel said, as Patience raced out of the door that afternoon.

It was Monday and the day of the auction had finally come. The days past had seemed to drag like the longest days of her life, as Patience had counted down the hours until next, she saw Caleb. How eager she had been to walk past the Smithson place, hoping to catch a glimpse of him, but her *mamm* had forbidden it. That morning, she had woken early, unable to sleep for her excitement and now she was about to make her way to the schoolhouse, eager to be at Caleb's side.

"I told her the other day," Barbara said, as Patience sighed and stopped in the doorway.

"Your hair is the covering of your head, not a fashionable accessory, Patience. I will not have you going out like that," Samuel continued, raising his eyebrows at her, and Patience sighed.

"I've got my kapp on," she complained, but her *daed* would hear none of it.

"Get yourself sorted out, Patience. I will not have the entire community speaking of you – and us, your parents – in reproachful ways. I am sure Caleb would not want to see you embarrassed," he said.

Reluctantly Patience allowed her *mamm* to tuck the loose strands of hair back beneath her kapp.

"Now, can I go?" she asked, and her parents nodded.

"Tell Annie we'll be there shortly," Barbara said, as Patience hurried out of the door.

She had wanted to look pretty for Caleb, though she knew her parent's opinions on the matter. Sometimes the rules she had to live by seemed so unfair and again she thought enviously of Eliza, who always seemed to look pretty, whatever the occasion.

The schoolhouse was already busy when she arrived, the school *kinner* performing a short pageant, a retelling of the story of Jonah and the Whale. Annie had worked hard, and the schoolhouse was decorated with bunting and banners, an array of cakes and refreshments laid out to one side, and the desks and chairs cleared away so that the auction could take place.

"Oh, I'm so glad you're here, Patience," Annie said, kissing her, as the *kinner* filed down from the makeshift stage at the front.

"Is Caleb here yet?" Patience asked, glancing around expectantly.

"Er... not yet, you mean the young man from the Smithson place?" Annie replied, sounding somewhat surprised by Patience's distracted tone.

"That's right. We had such a lovely walk on Friday, Annie. He was so kind and considerate. I invited him to come here today, I can't wait to see him," she said, and her sister nodded.

"Well, I'm sure he'll be here soon. You'll just have to keep an eye out for him, won't you. Excuse me, we're about to get started," Annie said.

Patience looked expectantly around the room.

Most of the community had turned out, Bishop Beiler and his wife Sarah had just arrived, but there was no sign of Caleb. Patience glanced up at the clock, which now said five minutes to the hour. Eliza and Matthew had also just arrived, and she hurried over to them, hoping that they might have seen Caleb and his uncle on their way to the schoolhouse.

"I thought he'd be here by now," she said, her heart fluttering, as she kissed Eliza on the cheek.

"We haven't seen him, I'm afraid, but I'm sure he'll be here," Eliza said.

Patience folded her arms as she tried to hide her disappointment.

"I got here early, especially," she said.

Eliza laughed. "Well, at least he's made you punctual for a change. Come on, the auction's about to start now," she said, taking Patience by the arm.

It was to be an auction of promises and Bishop Beiler had agreed to act as auctioneer. He banged a gavel down on the lectern which Annie had set up at the front of the schoolhouse and called them all to order.

"Well, good afternoon everyone, and wasn't that an excellent telling of the story of Jonah by the *kinner*? I particularly enjoyed little Reuben's depiction of the whale – quite terrifying. Now, I'm sure we all know why we're here – to raise money for the schoolhouse and to support Miss Graber in her efforts for the *kinner*. I must say that I've nothing but admiration for the work she does here and I'm glad to support this effort wholeheartedly. Now, lot number one is a promise from Mr. Jackson. He has pledged to mow an entire meadow once a month for the season – a very generous offer and one I'm sure will fetch a high price. Shall we start the bidding..." Bishop Beiler said, but Patience was now not listening.

She kept glancing at the door, willing it to open and for Caleb to appear. No doubt he was running late or had some business to attend to. That is what she told herself, wondering too if perhaps he were ill, the thought of which caused her panic to rise.

She had considered a dozen possible scenarios, barely listening to Bishop Beiler, when at last the door to the schoolhouse opened and she almost let out a cry of expectant delight. But her heart immediately fell when she saw it was Noah, entering alone, and slipping through the crowd, nodding to his new neighbors as he went.

"*Gut* day, Noah," Matthew whispered, as he came to stand next to them.

"I nearly didn't make it," he replied, "I lost track of time clearing the orchard."

"Isn't Caleb with you?" Patience asked, a look of despondency coming over her face.

"Oh, I'm not sure if he'll be here this afternoon," Noah replied, smiling at Patience, as Bishop Beiler banged his gavel down.

"A little attention, please," he said, raising an eyebrow at Patience, who blushed.

"It's getting a little close in here, I'm going to take some air," she whispered, and Eliza nodded.

Pushing her way through the crowded schoolhouse, she found some relief in the fresh air outside, crestfallen at the thought that Caleb had either forgotten their plans or else deliberately failed to come. Either way, it suggested that his words of the other day were less than sincere. It seemed that Eliza had been right to caution her, as much as it pained her to admit it.

"Are you all right, Miss Graber?" a voice behind her said, and she jumped, turning to find Noah standing behind her.

"Oh..." she began, embarrassed at the tears in her eyes, pulling out a handkerchief and dabbing her face.

"You know, you should be careful around Caleb," he said, and she looked at him in surprise.

"What do you mean?" she asked, wondering if he was teasing her again.

He sighed and shook his head. "It's complicated. But I know what he's like. I know you like him, but just don't let your heart get carried away. I'd hate to see you get hurt, that's all," he replied.

Patience found herself growing angry. It was always the same, her elders telling her what to do, and now it seemed that even her newest neighbor thought he knew best.

"I don't need to be told," she snapped, "besides, it was Caleb that didn't want to come here. He told me

I was the only reason he might come to like Faith's Creek."

She knew her words sounded hollow, the defense of a man who had failed to keep his word, but still she could not believe that Caleb had deliberately let her down, as much as reason told her otherwise.

Noah shrugged and nodded. "I just wanted to tell you, Patience, don't expect too much of him," he said, but Patience did not want to hear it and she excused herself, hurrying off along the lane in the direction of the Smithson place.

If Caleb would not come to her then she would go to Caleb. She would not be told anymore what was right for her. Now, she would decide what was right for her, whether it was or wasn't. She was tired of being told what to do and when to do it. She was old enough to make her own decisions, or so she told herself, and it seemed that everyone was conspiring against her. No longer would she be subject to the opinions of others, and right now, Patience wanted answers.

It was a sultry afternoon, and she was soon panting on the steep climb up to the Smithson farmstead.

She could see the trees in the orchard more clearly now, the brambles and creepers having been cut back and some of the grass mown over. She could not see Caleb anywhere and she let herself in through the gate, crossing the vegetable patch to where the barn stood, the doors propped open.

As she approached, she could hear voices coming from inside, and laughter – the laughter of a woman and Caleb's voice explaining some joke or other. Patience paused, wondering what was happening. She recognized the woman's voice, her flirtatious tone, and a lump rose in Patience's throat. With her whole body now trembling, she stepped forward, listening at the barn door, horrified by what she heard next.

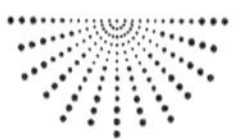

CHAPTER SEVEN

Caleb had just finished telling a joke and Patience listened, as the woman, who had been laughing in a most over-exaggerated way replied.

"You're so funny, Caleb, you really are," she said.

Now Patience knew why she recognized the voice. It was Esther Zook, a girl who had been in the same class as Patience at school, whose father ran the grocery store, and whose mother cleaned for Bishop Beiler. Now, Patience listened in astonishment to what came next, tears rolling down her cheeks.

"Do you know something, Esther? I'm so glad I met you, I don't know what Faith's Creek would be like without you. I think I'd just pack my things and go back to Ohio if I hadn't met you. You're a real find," Caleb said, and once again Esther giggled and told him he was quite something.

"And I'm so glad you came here, too. It's such a dull place and I've been waiting so long to meet a man like you," Esther replied.

She had always been a silly, flirtatious girl, and Patience had often heard her *mamm* speak of Esther in less than glowing terms.

"That girl will come to a bad end," she would say when rumors of Esther's flirtatious ways were circulating around the community.

"Well, I'm glad we met, too," Caleb replied, and Esther giggled.

Patience imagined him touching her face, just as he had done to her down by the creek. Tears flowed down her cheeks, and she turned to flee, hurrying through the garden, out of the gate, and down the lane, anxious to get as far away as possible from Caleb and Esther. The pain in her heart was outdone by how much she felt like a fool... an utter fool.

She did not want to return to the schoolhouse, knowing what Eliza and Annie would say when they heard what had happened. It embarrassed her to think of how easily she had been led on by Caleb, fooled into thinking that he liked her, when all along he was just playing her for a fool. How many other women had he tricked, she wondered, making her way instead toward the creek, and sitting down sadly beneath a tree at the water's edge.

Picking up a stone, she skimmed it across the water, watching it splash, thinking of Caleb. She had placed him on a pedestal, invested all her hopes in him, and now those hopes had been dashed. It was a sad day and Patience felt a fool for being so caught up in the fantasy of what might have been. Her sisters had warned her, her *mamm* had warned her, even Caleb's own uncle had warned her, and she still had not listened. She was pondering this when the sound of footsteps caused her to look up.

It was Noah, a spike of anger rushed through her at the thought that he had followed her. She wanted nothing more to do with the King family, for as far as Patience was concerned, she would be happy to see them return to Ohio and never darken Faith's Creek again. Noah waved to her, hurrying over, and smiling, sitting down without invitation and looking at her, shaking his head and sighing.

"I tried to warn you," he said.

Patience made a face. "Have you been following me?" she demanded.

The older man blushed. "I just wanted to make sure you were all right. I knew what you'd find up at the house. That young girl was just arriving as I left. I think Caleb must have met her at the store or something. Anyway, I'm sorry you had to see that, Caleb has a habit of it," he said.

Patience felt the tears rising in her eyes. "He does?" she asked.

Noah nodded. "We didn't just move here for the soil. Back in Ohio, Caleb had something of a reputation amongst our neighbors. Things were growing awkward. I thought that perhaps a new start in a new place would do him good. But it seems that he brought his old habits with him, more's the pity," Noah said, shaking his head again.

"But I overheard him tell Esther how much he liked

her. It was exactly the same as he told me the other day," she said, brushing away her tears.

"And he'll tell some other poor girl the same thing next week and the week after, no doubt until our reputation here is the same as it was back in Ohio. I fear for him, Patience, I really do. I've always tried to instill values in him, the sort of values that our community stands for. But ever since his rumspringa, Caleb's wanted something else. He'll never be content growing vegetables and planting crops, his heart's somewhere else. That's why I tried to warn you about him," Noah said.

Patience gave him a weak smile. "I'm sorry I didn't listen. I didn't listen to anyone. Not you, not my sisters, not my *mamm* or *daed*. I got so caught up in my dreams that the reality of it didn't hit me," Patience said, knowing that now she had had a full dose of reality, a reality that hurt.

"Don't be too harsh on yourself. You wouldn't be the first girl to be caught up in Caleb's advances. And you're certainly not the first in history to make such a mistake," Noah said, smiling sympathetically at her.

"I was a fool to think that a boy like Caleb would be

interested in me. I'm just a plain Jane, but I got so worked up over him I didn't think straight," Patience replied.

She really felt a fool, and she was dreading the truth being revealed to her sisters and parents. They would all say "we told you so," but it would be Patience who would remain miserable and still without the husband she had always dreamed of.

"Don't blame yourself. It's Caleb that's the problem, not you. And I can promise you one thing, Esther Zook will be feeling just the same as you do by next week. He's probably already got his eyes on another woman in Faith's Creek. He treats women like a pair of socks, worn for a day then discarded into the wash," Noah said, shaking his head.

He seemed genuinely upset by his nephew's actions, eager to make amends, and Patience could not help but be drawn by his kindly demeanor. She had stopped crying now, her sorrow replaced by a sense of righteous anger against Caleb. How dare he treat women in such a way, as though they were objects to be discarded at his whim. Perhaps she had been saved from an unfortunate fate and she was grateful to Noah for having searched her out to warn her, even though at first those warnings had gone unheeded.

"My sisters will tell me I was wrong to get so caught up in it all," she said, shaking her head.

Noah nodded. "I'm sure they just want the best for you. Eliza's such a lovely woman and I stand by what I said, Faith's Creek has welcomed us with open arms. That's why it disappoints me to have Caleb behaving like this. I don't want us to get the same reputation here as in Ohio," he said, shaking his head.

"But you won't be tarred with the same brush. It's Caleb that's in the wrong," Patience replied, rising to her feet and sighing.

"May I walk you home?" he asked.

She nodded, glad of the company. "I have to face them at some point," she said, and he smiled, offering her his arm.

They walked along the lane and took the shortcut across the cornfields. Patience was surprised how easy she found him to talk to, his kindness shining through. He listened to her, too, more so than anyone else ever had. Patience was used to being dismissed as the younger sister, barely acknowledged and never asked to state her opinion. But here was a man who seemed genuinely interested in her and Patience felt some consolation in the hurt that she had experienced.

"You know, I didn't mean to tease you the other night at dinner when you broke the plate. I'm sorry if I upset you," he said, as they walked through the corn.

Patience blushed at the reminder of her clumsiness, thinking back to the accident with the jam jar when Noah had come to her aid the first time.

"You didn't. I should have been more careful," she replied, smiling at him.

"I find myself daydreaming sometimes, especially since my wife died," he said, his tone becoming somber, as though returning to memories he found hard to dwell on.

"What was she like?" Patience asked, curious to learn more about their new neighbor, who seemed so different from his nephew.

While Caleb appeared immature and flirtatious,

brash and sure of himself, Noah was quite the opposite. A quiet and contemplative man, who gave thought to every word he uttered and radiated a gentle kindness which Patience found endearing.

"We weren't married for long. A fever took her, and we buried her ten years ago. I think about her every day and I've spent the years since hoping to find a woman as decent and kind as she was, someone to start over again with. It's not easy when your nephew gives you a reputation the same as his. Back in Ohio, there wasn't a woman who'd look at me, they'd all say I was just like Caleb or worse, that it was me he learned it from," Noah said, shaking his head sadly.

Patience frowned, she could not believe that Noah was anything like Caleb and she looked up at him and smiled.

"You're nothing like him and if he'd taken after your example, then perhaps he'd have found someone to settle down with," she said.

As she looked up at him, it was like seeing him in a different light. There was something about him that drew her to him, a quality such as other men did not have, such as she had not experienced before. But there was a sadness about him, too. A longing for something he had lost, the love of a woman. Patience could not help but feel sorry for him, hoping that she could be a friend to him as he had been to her. They had reached her house now, and Patience could see her *mamm* and *daed* through the kitchen window. Noah tipped his hat to them, the two of them waving, as he bid Patience goodbye.

"I hope you'll be all right, now," he said.

She nodded. "I'll know not to trust Caleb, that's for certain," she replied.

"Just so long as you know his uncle's quite different," he said.

"I can see that," she replied, and he nodded to her, before departing down the lane, waving to her from the corner, where the tall corn sheafs obscured the further view.

"That was nice of Noah to walk you home, Patience. What happened to Caleb?" her *mamm* asked a few moments later when Patience had stepped into the kitchen.

"Oh, he wasn't what I thought he was," she said, excusing herself and hurrying upstairs.

Her parents had looked at one another in surprise, but Patience had offered no further explanation. Her thoughts turned to Noah. In her bedroom, with the door closed, she kneeled down by her bed and prayed to *Gott* for guidance – would her prayers be answered now? No longer did she beg *Gott* to send her a man to marry, but to show her what was right for her and her alone.

"Show me the way," she whispered, and it was the face of Noah, not of Caleb, that came to mind.

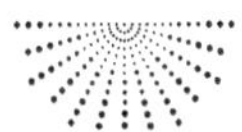

CHAPTER EIGHT

The next morning, Patience awoke to the sound of her *mamm* calling to her. She realized she had slept in and leaped out of bed, hurrying downstairs, where her parents sat waiting. She had promised to help her *daed* in the garden that day, for he was intending to harvest the early potato crop ready for market.

"Didn't you want to help?" he asked, putting on his straw hat, as Patience poured herself a cup of coffee.

"I'm sorry, *Daed*, I was so tired after yesterday," she replied, yawning as she spoke.

"We didn't even see you at the auction, Eliza said

you ran off as soon as it began. What must Bishop Beiler have thought?" Barbara said, tutting at her.

"I just needed some air," Patience said, as her *daed* stepped out of the door onto the porch.

"Come and help me when you're ready, Patience," he called back.

Patience nodded through a mouthful of bread and butter.

"Were you upset about something last night, Patience?" her mamm asked.

Patience was not in the mood for explanations. She had resolved to push any thoughts of Caleb aside and in doing so, she had found peace in the thought that no man should have a hold so strong over her. She had realized that it was infatuation, not genuine feeling, that had drawn her to Caleb and how glad she was that the truth about him had been revealed.

"I might take a walk over to Eliza's when I've finished helping *Daed*," she said, putting on her kapp and kissing her *mamm* on the cheek.

"All right, but be back for dinner, you hear me?" Barbara called out, but Patience was already gone.

She felt a draw to visit Noah, his kindly words and gentle demeanor were such a contrast to Caleb's overbearing flirtatiousness. He had made no demands on her and for the first time in her life, it had felt as though someone had listened to her. Now, she hung awkwardly by the vegetable patch, her *daed* looking up at her and frowning.

"You usually enjoy helping me with the harvest, Patience. What's wrong with you today?" he asked.

Patience shrugged. "I'm sorry, *Daed,* I just don't feel like it today," she said.

"Do you think I feel like it? Do you think I feel like it when it rains and the wind blows across the cornfields and I have to be out in all weathers growing vegetables and looking after the animals? We all have to do things we don't feel like sometimes, Patience. That's how life is," he said but the smile he gave her let her know that he was teasing.

Reluctantly, she kneeled down and took up a trowel, digging up the new potatoes from the ground, shaking off the dirt, and tossing them into her *daed's* basket.

"Did you ever wonder about leaving Faith's Creek?" she asked.

He looked at her in surprise. "Oh, so this is what it's all about, is it? You had your rumspringa, you made your decision," he began, a look of worry lining his face.

Patience shook her head. "I don't mean that. I'm just curious about other people, that's all. Like the Kings, they left Ohio to come here. It must have been a big decision, don't you think?" she asked.

Her *daed* nodded. "I can't imagine ever leaving Faith's Creek, but some people do. I hope you won't though," he said.

Patience smiled. "I won't," she replied.

They soon had a fair crop of potatoes, enough to portion into brown paper bags ready to be sold by the pound at the market next week. Samuel Graber's vegetable stall was a favorite amongst the residents of Faith's Creek. His carrots and leeks were prize winners and he had grown the largest turnip in Pennsylvania, or so it was claimed. With the potato crop dug, Patience was allowed to go for her walk, telling her *dead* she was going to visit Eliza, to which he replied that she was to remind Matthew *again* to collect his tomato plant seeds.

"And tell her to remember to water those dahlias she planted, else there'll be no flowers to cut for the flower festival," he called out, as Patience hurried down the lane.

But she was not going to visit Eliza, despite feeling guilty for the fact of lying to her parents as to her true motives. Instead, she was going to visit Noah up at the Smithson place, hoping to thank him once again for walking her home and to apologize for at first thinking him rude for making fun of her.

It was another hot day, the cloudless sky above blue and hazy, and even at this early hour, it was shimmering across the cornfields. Patience thought of swimming in the creek or of lazing in the garden drinking lemonade. Faith's Creek always looked its best in the sunshine and she waved to several of their neighbors as she made her way through the cornfields and then onto the lane up to the farmstead.

Nervously, Patience looked around for any signs of Eliza or Matthew. She did not want her deception to be revealed, but the draw of seeing Noah was too great. She hurried on up the hill, pausing outside the gate, hot and breathless. It was Caleb that she saw first, ducking back, she tried to hide behind a tree but failed. He hailed to her and she had no choice but to approach him.

"Patience, I'm sorry about yesterday. I was so busy up here in the garden that I quite lost track of time. I was all set to come and then I looked at the clock and it said five o'clock, I was so angry with myself. Say, why don't we take another walk together this afternoon, or tomorrow if you're not busy," he said, evidently believing she had come with the intention of seeing him.

"No thank you, Caleb," she said, hoping that her voice sounded suitably curt and cold.

He looked at her in surprise, taking off his straw hat and pulling out a handkerchief to mop his brow.

"Are you busy, then?" he asked.

She shook her head feeling a strange sense of accomplishment. "Not at all, I just don't want to go for a walk with you. Excuse me, but I'm looking for your uncle," she replied, and hurried off across the garden toward the orchard, leaving an astonished Caleb behind.

Noah was up a ladder on the far side of the orchard. He was chopping back brambles that had engulfed a gnarly old apple tree, the first fruits of which were budding, promising a fine crop in the fall. As Patience approached, he looked up in surprise and smiled, waving to her, before climbing down the ladder and coming to meet her.

"Well, this is a nice surprise. I was just cutting back the brambles," he said.

Patience smiled. "I can't believe what you've done here already, it looks so nice. I didn't realize how many trees there were," she said, looking around her.

Not only had Abraham Smithson planted apple trees but pear, quince, and damson, too. Now, the trees had been revealed, the branches chopped back, and the grass below mown. It was a little paradise and Patience could happily have sat beneath the trees for hours, as the birds sang above, and bees buzzing in the flowers which grew in the hedgerow surrounding the orchard.

"There's still a lot to do, but we'll get there," he said, still smiling at her.

"Well, I wanted to thank you," she said, and he looked at her curiously.

"You've nothing to thank me for," he said, but she shook her head.

"Oh, I meant for walking me home yesterday. It was sweet of you, and for telling me what I needed to hear, about Caleb, I mean," she said, glancing over her shoulder to where Caleb was working in the garden.

"You don't need to thank me for that, but I'm glad you took heed of it," he said.

"I've made my feelings clear to him. And I'm sorry if I thought you rude at first for your little joke. I know it was only made in jest," she said, blushing, as he laughed.

"I do like my little jokes. But I'm sorry if I made it at your expense," he replied.

There was a pause now, and Patience wondered what to say. He was such a genuine man, a contrast to his nephew who seemed to exist behind a veneer of lies. He smiled at her, and she found herself blurting out an unconsidered invitation, though one she had been thinking of as she crossed the cornfields earlier that morning.

"Will you have dinner with us tonight?" she asked.

Noah looked at her in surprise. "Well, that would be very nice. Did your *mamm* and *daed* invite me?" he asked, and she shook her head.

"*Nee*, but they'll be happy to have you there, I know they will. We just dug up a whole load of new potatoes fresh from the soil this morning. You won't taste any better in all of Faith's Creek, and my *mamm's* a wonderful cook. You should taste her apple strudel, it's quite something. Please say you'll come," she said.

Noah nodded. "I'd be delighted. So long as it's no trouble to your parents," he replied, but Patience was not thinking of her parents, only of her happiness at the thought of sharing dinner with Noah that evening.

"Then seven o'clock," she said, blushing again, before bidding him goodbye and hurrying off back through the orchard.

As she came through the garden, Caleb looked up and scowled at her, but she avoided his gaze, not even acknowledging him, as she opened the gate and stepped back out into the lane. Her heart was beating fast, not because of Caleb's gaze, but because of Noah's acceptance and she thanked *Gott* for this new friendship and all that it might bring.

CHAPTER NINE

*B*arbara was surprised to be informed that there would be an extra guest for dinner that night, not least because she had thought that Patience was visiting Eliza, rather than Noah King.

"You should have asked before inviting someone to dinner, Patience... but we can hardly retract the invitation now," she said.

Patience blushed. "I just wanted to thank him for walking me home, that's all," Patience said.

Barbara chuckled. "I understand, but it's polite to ask the person who'll cook the dinner if they're happy to do so, Patience. Never mind, you can help me. I'll make an apple strudel and we'll have pork schnitzel and new potatoes, go and tell your *daed* to cut me some leeks, that'll make a nice vegetable to go with it. Hurry up now, we've got a lot to do," she said, and the two of them set to work.

Samuel Graber was equally surprised to learn that they were to have a guest for dinner, but when the appointed hour came, he greeted Noah warmly. The two men immediately began to discuss crop rotations and how best to manage the orchard. Noah was just 10 years younger than Patience's daed, and it seemed that the two of them would get along very well. Annie was there, too, and she had been pleased to report that the auction had raised nearly $600 for the schoolhouse.

"Bishop Beiler made a further donation to round it up," Annie said, as Patience placed a dish of potatoes on the table.

"We're proud of you, Annie, you've worked so hard," Barbara said, as she handed round the plates.

"This is a veritable feast, Mrs. Graber. I'm so very grateful to you," Noah said, taking up his knife and fork after they had saidgrace.

"It's just good old-fashioned cooking, that's what I do best," she said, and the family tucked in hungrily.

The conversation mainly concerned the farmstead, Noah and Samuel exchanged advice with one another, with Barbara interjecting occasionally with her own opinion. Patience sat quietly. It was enough to be in Noah's company, his warmth and friendliness evident for all to see.

"And I'm thinking of planting some gooseberry bushes, too. Do you think they'd be popular on the market?" he asked.

Barbara nodded. "I'd make a fool with them, a little cream and sugar, lemon rind and a sprig of elderflower, delicious," she said.

Noah smiled. "Then you'll have the first punnet," he said, glancing at Patience, who smiled back at him.

"I'll come and help you plant them out. I love the thought of bringing that wild old orchard back to life," she said.

Samuel raised his eyebrows and chuckled. "Why is it when I try to get you to weed or plant out you've always got something else to be doing," he asked.

Patience blushed. "I just thought I could help," she replied.

"I'd be delighted to have the help," Noah said.

Patience felt as if the sun was shining down just for her.

"Shall I show you what I've got out in the small holding? I think you'll be impressed," Samuel said, rising from the table, "we'll be back in a moment, Barbara, just in time for some of your excellent apple strudel."

Samuel led Noah outside, leaving Patience with her *mamm* and Annie. As soon as the porch door swung shut, Barbara rounded on her, a look of astonishment on her face. Patience was quite taken aback, and she glanced at Annie, who shook her head, the two of them waiting for their *mamm* to speak.

"Just what do you think you're doing, Patience? I thought it was Caleb that you liked. One moment all we hear about is Caleb this and Caleb that, but now you've forgotten him and it's his uncle you seem interested in. Are you thinking of courting him?" she asked.

Patience felt her face flush red as a beet. "I... but *Mamm*, I just wanted to thank him for his kindness," she replied.

She had no desire to tell her *mamm* the true reason she had rejected Caleb, knowing the damage it would do to his reputation and to that of Noah. It was best to forget the whole thing and move on, which was exactly what she was trying to do.

"Are you really thinking of courting Noah?" Annie asked.

Patience looked at her in confusion. *Was she?* "I... I don't know what I want. Maybe I'm getting ahead of myself. I always do, I always think I know what's best but I guess... I just get so lonely. Sometimes all I want is a family of my own and yet no one ever seems to want to talk to me, to listen to me... Noah did." Tears rose in her eyes.

Annie reached out and took her hand. "He's ten years your senior, ten years your daed's junior," Barbara said.

Annie looked up sharply. "I think we should give Patience some credit, *Mamm*. She's old enough to make her own decisions now, I know that in the past she's been somewhat immature over men." Annie glanced at Patience who began to protest.

"I haven't..." she began, but her sister stopped her.

"But now, that romantic streak might have been doused with a little reality and it's clear that Mr. King is a kind and decent man with a good reputation. Which is more than can be said about his nephew," she said, glancing at Patience.

"Well, I don't deny that he's a delightful man, I just wonder if he's right for Patience," Barbara replied, but once again Annie leaped to Patience's defense.

"And you and *Daed* aren't exactly matched in age, are you?" she said, to which their *mamm* now blushed.

"Well, no," she replied.

In fact, there was almost fifteen years difference between Barbara and Samuel Graber, but that had not prevented the two of them from enjoying a long and happy marriage together as the very best of friends. Patience glanced at her mother, wondering now what her own feelings truly were. It had all happened so quickly, and she worried that this might again be infatuation rather than genuine feeling. But in the past, Patience would never have imagined that a man like Noah could be the one for her. Annie was right. She had been quick to let romantic notions overtake her, and slow to see that true love and affection could come at the most unexpected of times.

"Exactly, and look at your marriage," Annie continued, "it's a model of what every marriage should be, filled with love and mutual respect, blessed by *Gott* and given as an example to us all. Maybe Patience's patience has finally born fruit."

Barbara looked at them both and smiled. All three of the sisters had always been close to her, and she was as much a friend to them as she was a *mamm* and a parent. Now, she looked at Patience, and sighed, reaching out and taking her by the hand.

"My girls have grown up, they're not my little *bopplies* anymore. They're women and I'm proud of each of you. You're right, Annie, it's time we let Patience make her own decisions. I'm proud that she's making these decisions and thinking of someone with whom she might build a real future. That's what I want for you all and if Noah King is the right man for you, then so be it, though once again I caution the speed that this has come at. Be sure of your heart, Patience and the only way to do that is by praying to *Gott* and asking for guidance," she said.

Patience smiled. "I will do, *Mamm*," she said, rising to her feet and putting her arms around her *mamm*, who kissed her on both cheeks, just as the porch door opened and Noah and Samuel returned.

"It's quite some vegetable patch your *daed's* got there," Noah said, sitting down next to Patience and shaking his head.

"You'll soon have that farmstead producing more fruit and vegetables than you can sell," Samuel said, as Barbara served up the apple strudel.

"Then I can go and help up there?" Patience asked.

Samuel nodded. "You can, so long as you help me here, too," he replied with a chuckle.

Patience grinned, hopeful that this might be the beginning of something very special indeed.

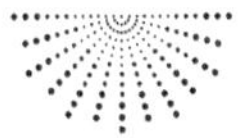

CHAPTER TEN

The days that followed were like bliss, Patience helped Noah in the orchard and the two of them went for long walks by the creek and up into the woods along the ridge above the farmstead. It was everything she had ever dreamed of and the more time she spent with him, the more she became enamored with him. It was a week after he had taken dinner with her parents, and Noah had invited Patience to join him on a picnic by the creek. Her *mamm* had packed a meat pie and some sandwiches for them, along with a cake and some bottles of ginger beer. Patience had the basket in hand and was hurrying to meet Noah by the fork in the lane.

"What a beautiful day it is," Noah said, as she met him, and he offered her his arm, the two of them walking happily together in the sunshine.

"I think my *mamm* had packed enough food for a church outing," Patience said, as Noah offered to take the basket from her.

They made their way along the lane and through the meadow toward the path by the water's edge, talking happily about this and that. Patience felt as though she did not have a care in the world, so taken up was she in Noah's company. They walked by the water for about half a mile, before finding a shady spot to lay out the rug which Noah had brought, along with his own contribution to the picnic.

"I'm not much of a cook, but we've got some apples that were stored up in one of the barns, they're tart but delicious and I've bought us a cake from Katy Zook's stall. It's chocolate," he said, taking it out of a bag and placing it on the rug.

"It looks delicious. Isn't it lovely here? We used to swim in the creek here as children. Annie never would, she was always reading, but Eliza and I used to splash her," Patience said, fondly recalling the memories of her childhood.

"I haven't swum in years, though Eve and I used to do so back in Ohio when we were younger. There was a creek just like this and I remember swimming out to a little island together and sitting watching the sunset. After we were married, of course," he said, smiling at Patience, as she laid out the picnic things.

"What was she like? Eve, I mean?" she asked, for she had been curious about Noah's wife, though unsure of whether it was appropriate to ask about her.

"She was a delight, though I always seemed to say the wrong things when we were courting. I've a habit of that, as you know," he said, shaking his head.

"I can't imagine what it must have been like for you when she died," Patience said, her heart going out to him.

"It was hard, I don't think you ever get over something like that. You just learn to live with it and the days become easier. But there isn't a day that goes by when I don't think of her and honor her memory," he said, opening a bottle of ginger beer.

"Did you have anyone there for you?" she asked, and he nodded, offering her a glass.

"My brother – Caleb's father – he was a real rock for me. He pulled me out of my sorrow and made me live again. He showed me that things would be all right. It was him that got me interested in growing things. I always think that when you grow something it's like giving life to the world, making it just a little more beautiful. I promised to take care of Caleb, though I haven't done a very good job of it, have I?" he said, sighing and shaking his head.

Patience reached out and placed her hand on his arm. She felt so sorry for him, for his life had not been short of a tragedy.

"Don't blame yourself for Caleb's faults. He'll settle down eventually, I just hope he doesn't hurt anyone else in the process. But you're not responsible for what he chooses to do, only for what you try and teach him, and it seems you've taught him just fine," she said, cutting a wedge of meat pie and putting it on a plate for him.

"You're very kind, Patience," he said, taking the plate from her and beginning to eat.

"It's the truth, he'll work himself out, we've all got our foibles. I know I have," she said, unwrapping a ham and tomato sandwich.

Her *mamm* had cut the bread thickly and spread it with lots of butter, just how Patience liked it, and she took a large bite, smiling at Noah, who laughed.

"Your *mamm* knows how to pack a picnic. But I don't think you've any foibles, you're just about perfect" he said.

Patience blushed. She could think of a dozen reasons why she was not perfect, most of them with regards to her romantic leanings. Patience did not live up to her name, and her biggest fault lay in rushing head on without thinking of the consequences. This picnic, everything that had happened was a case in point, and she wondered again if she was doing the right thing.

"I always imagined I'd be swept off my feet by a handsome young man and live happily ever after, but now I see things differently," she admitted, embarrassed to voice such a ridiculous notion.

But it was true, that was what she had always believed, and now she regretted such romanticized leanings. They had only led to Caleb, and Caleb had led to unhappiness. She was so grateful to Noah for leading her back along the right path and preventing her from falling into something terrible, a regret she would have been forced to endure her whole life long.

"What do you mean?" he asked.

"It's like a fairytale, but it's not real life, there's no happily ever after in real life," she said, shaking her head.

"But there can be contentment ever after. You're right, no one lives without troubles. I know that well enough, but we all deserve to find what brings us happiness, even if there's a bumpy ride along the way. That's what I keep telling myself," he said, setting down his glass of ginger beer and smiling at her.

"That's just what I need to hear," she said, moving a little closer to him, her hand reaching out to his.

Patience gazed into his eyes. No longer did she see an older man or a man who did not fit her ideal, but a man who possessed all the qualities that went beyond the superficial, a man with integrity and honor, kindness and compassion. A man who had been there for her when she needed it most. Now, he smiled at her, leaning forward, their lips poised to meet in a kiss.

"Uncle Noah, I've been looking all over for you," Caleb called out, and Patience looked up, startled by the sight of the young man hurrying toward them.

She turned away in embarrassment, as Noah leaped to his feet, evidently angered at being interrupted.

"I don't need to account for my movements every moment of the day, Caleb," he said, but his nephew only laughed.

"Oh, I see what's going on. Why are you out here trying to woo Miss Graber? You're twice her age, and only half as pretty," he said.

Noah's face fell.

But Patience was having none of it. She was angry now, Caleb's mocking tone an insult to the uncle who had given up so much to take care of him. She folded her arms and scowled at him, as Noah began to stutter.

"I wasn't... just you wait, now, Caleb," he began, but

now it seemed that his nerves had taken hold and he shook his head, glancing at Patience and then back to Caleb.

"A picnic, it's all very cozy here," Caleb continued, still mocking his uncle, and now Noah picked up his things and shook his head.

"I'm sorry, Patience, I didn't mean to embarrass you. *Gut* day," he said turning to leave.

"I don't want you to go," Patience called after him.

Caleb's eyes widened in surprise. "Oh, I see, you're doing this to get back at me? Because I didn't come to the auction. I told you, I forgot about it, I lost track of time," he began.

Patience shook her head. "It might not have occurred to you, Caleb, but the whole world doesn't revolve around you and what you want. Besides, we both know that you missed the auction for a very different reason," she said.

Caleb's eyes widened even more and his mouth dropped open in horror. "What?" he said.

She nodded. "Yes, you lost track of time with Esther

Zook, not the garden," she said. "Don't worry, you are not the first."

Caleb swallowed hard and took a step back.

Noah had been about to flee, but he paused, looking at Caleb and shaking his head. "You brought this on yourself, Caleb, no one else did it," he said

Caleb looked around angrily. "And what do you think she sees in you?" he asked.

Noah sighed. "I don't know, but I hope some integrity."

"I see a real man, Caleb, one who is kind and gentle, caring and loyal, a man that does what's right by a woman and doesn't lead her down the garden path like a fool. I was foolish and naïve to believe all those things you told me. Well, I won't make that mistake again," she said, fixing him with a hard stare.

"I meant what I said," Caleb replied, now sounding defensive.

Patience laughed. "I'm sure you meant it in the moment, Caleb, but then you meant it with Esther Zook, too. And I wonder how many other women have heard those same words and believed them. I won't be fooled again. Where were you at the auction? When you promised to meet me. You were flirting with Esther, that's where, and now you think you can snatch me back with a few well-chosen words? Well, I've got news for you... you can't," she said, astonished at the force that anger gave to her words.

There was a time when Patience would have let herself be walked over when she would have accepted his behavior in the desperate hope of securing his affections. But those days were over. She had grown up and realized that her own happily ever after was more than a handsome man who thought himself to be deserving of a woman's affections, but instead, it was a man with integrity and honor, a man who treated her with respect, a man like Noah King.

"Oh, I see, you're just trying to get back at me, aren't you? You're not interested in my uncle at all. You just want revenge," Caleb cried.

Noah raised his hand. "That's enough, Caleb, I won't hear you insult Patience like that."

Caleb turned to his uncle in astonishment. "Do you

really think she's interested in courting a man like you?" he asked.

Patience nodded. "Oh, I'm very interested in doing so and I'll tell you something. Caleb King, you've got a lot of growing up to do before you learn what true love means," she said, slipping her hand into Noah's.

At this, she felt him grown tense, his hand trembling, but she squeezed it tight, the two of them facing Caleb, who now shook his head and turned away.

"You don't mean a word of it," he growled, but there was something in his voice, as though he could not entirely believe his own words.

"Maybe in time you'll settle down, Caleb, and learn how to treat a woman right," Patience said, "but I don't want someone halfhearted, someone, that would cast me aside when his attentions are turned. No, I want a man I can trust, a man like your uncle. I can't wait for that, I can't wait for you or anyone else to grow up, you hear me? I want to find that person, now, and I've found it with your uncle, from whom you could learn a thing or two." She was looking at Noah, who seemed astonished by her words.

Caleb only shook his head, still scowling at them

both, but it was clear that he knew he was beaten, his own words and admonitions sounding hollow and making him appear foolish. With a final glance at them both, he turned on his heel and stomped off through the trees, leaving Patience and Noah alone. She linked her hand with his and turned to him, smiling, though wondering if she had overstepped the mark. Did he feel for her what she felt for him?

"I'm so sorry for his behavior, Patience. If I'd known he was going to do that I'd never have brought you down here," Noah began.

Patience shook her head and shushed him. "You couldn't have known he was going to do that. He's young and immature, and there were some things he just had to be told. Who knows, maybe he'll learn from it, and treat Esther, or whoever else, right from now on," Patience replied.

"And I'm sorry if I overstepped the mark with all this," Noah said, pointing down to the remnants of the picnic.

"What do you mean? I was having a lovely time until he came along and spoiled it. Here. Let's have another glass of ginger beer and a slice of cake. We don't need to let our afternoon be spoiled by him," Patience said, settling herself back down on the rug.

Noah sat down next to her and smiled. He put his hand in hers, their eyes meeting and Patience felt her heart skip a beat. She felt drawn to him, as though this moment was always meant to be. It was like an answer to her prayers, though in that mysterious way in which Bishop Beiler so often spoke of *Gott* working.

"I don't know what to say, except to ask if you truly meant what you said back there," Noah said.

Patience nodded. "I meant every word of it. I'm not always clumsy, especially when it comes to words," she said.

Noah looked deep into her eyes. "I wasn't expecting to meet someone like you, not so soon. It just goes to show that when you don't look, you find. I'm so glad I met you and I know we haven't known one another long, but there's something about you. As though all this was meant to be," he said, and leaning forward, he brought his lips to hers, the two of them sharing a sweet, brief kiss that sent a shiver down Patience's spine.

She had always imagined her first kiss, though it was nothing like this. There was nothing that could have prepared her for what she felt, caught up as she was in that perfect moment. As their lips parted, Patience realized that she had found everything she had always dreamed of, but in an entirely unexpected way.

"Does this mean...?" she asked.

He nodded. "If it's what you want, then it's what I want to," he said, their lips meeting once again.

Noah pulled back. "Your parents would kill me if they knew what we had just done."

Patience blushed. She knew that such a kiss was not unheard of before marriage but she also knew that her mamm would be disappointed. "I'm sorry," she said.

Noah ran a finger down her cheek and cupped her jaw, staring into her eyes. "Never be sorry. I love you Patience. I think I have loved you since the first time

I set eyes on you. Make me the happiest man in Faith's Creek by becoming my *fraa*."

"*Jah*, Of course, I will. I love you too Noah."

Once more they kissed, a sweet, chaste kiss before they drew apart to continue with the picnic. The atmosphere was now one of celebration and love.

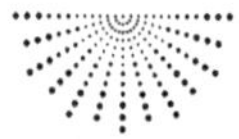

CHAPTER ELEVEN

Four months later

Patience finished sweeping the kitchen. The old Smithson place was looking tidy and respectable, now that it had a woman's touch. Patience looked around proudly at the home she had made for herself and Noah. They had been married for precisely a month, and it had been the happiest month of Patience's life. She felt as though she had everything she had ever dreamed of – a loving husband and a home to call her own.

Now, she checked on her kapp and put on a shawl, taking up an apple pie she had baked that morning and setting off through the garden and down the lane to visit with Eliza and Matthew. The garden was looking neat and tidy and Noah was out in the orchard, cutting back the trees after the last of the windfalls had been collected. It was fall now, and the landscape was a sea of golden reds, the cornfields mowed back and the trees on the turn. Patience breathed in the fresh air, pinching herself that her dreams had finally come true.

Her sister was out in the yard feeding the chickens when Patience came up the lane. Eliza put down her bowl of corn and came to meet her at the gate. There was a glow to Eliza, a wonderful sense of happiness that she exuded, maybe because she had just discovered she was with child. All three sisters were ecstatic at the prospect of welcoming the next generation into the family.

Patience embraced Eliza, kissing her on both cheeks and handing her the pie, which was still warm from the oven.

"Oh, you shouldn't have, but it smells delicious," Eliza said, as the two sisters walked up the porch steps and into the house.

"Well, I thought you'd have so much to do and I know Matthew likes an apple pie," Patience replied.

"Matthew likes anything sweet. He'll love it, *denke*, Patience. Why don't you sit down and I'll make us some coffee?" Eliza said, pointing to Patience's usual chair.

Ever since she had been married, Patience had noticed how differently her sister now treated her, how differently everyone treated her. No longer was she merely a girl to be talked down to or assumed not to know what was best for her, instead, she was an equal, given responsibility, and asked for her opinion.

"You're not overdoing it, are you?" Patience asked.

Eliza shook her head. "Everyone keeps asking that, I had *Mamm* here earlier on fussing over me. But I'm fine, I'm just looking forward to the *boppli* arriving... but it's still so many months away, though," she said, putting a kettle on the stove to boil.

"Is Matthew still working on the nursery?" Patience asked, glancing through a door at the far end of the kitchen, where tins of paint and rolls of wallpaper lay on the floor.

"He's in there every night, he wants it to be just perfect for his little girl," Eliza replied.

"Or boy," Patience said, and her sister laughed.

"He's convinced it's a girl, I'm not worried either way, so long as it's healthy and grows up to be *Gott* loving," she said.

There was freshly baked seed cake to go with their coffee and the sisters enjoyed catching up and talking about life in the community.

"Noah's nearly finished cutting back all the trees ready for winter. We've got a whole barn full of windfalls, we'll have to get them dried or stored before the winter sets in," Patience said, finishing her drink.

"I've never seen you looking so happy, Patience. It warms my heart, it really does," Eliza said, smiling at her, as she took her empty cup.

"He's so kind and considerate, Eliza, just like Matthew. Every day he tells me he loves me, I know he means it with all his heart," she said, still not able to believe that she had found the man she had so long dreamed of.

"It was an answer to prayer, Patience, maybe not the

prayer you prayed, but certainly the one the rest of us did," Eliza said.

Patience looked at her curiously. "What prayer was that?" she asked, for she had not realized that others had been praying for her.

"Just a simple prayer, which I always think are the best. We prayed for you to be happy and to be freed from this restlessness," she replied, "and it seems that prayer was answered."

The two sisters sat a while longer and when Patience bid Eliza goodbye, they promised to visit again very soon. Patience set off up the lane toward home, glancing back over the fields toward her parent's house, and thinking how strange it was to no longer live there but to have her own responsibilities, the responsibilities she had always dreamed of. Only Annie remained with their *mamm* and *daed* and Patience wondered if she would ever find a husband or be forever wedded to her work.

"Oh, there you are, I was just about to send out a search party," Noah said when Patience let herself in through the gate a short while later.

"You know how it is, when we sisters get together there's no stopping us," Patience replied.

Noah laughed. "Let's have something to eat and then you can help me out in the orchard, I need someone to hold the ladder while I cut the top branches from the tress. I don't trust my balance," he said, taking her by the hand and leading her inside.

There were bread and cheese for their meal, some apple juice from their first pressing, and a cherry pie for dessert. When Noah had finished eating, he sat back and sighed, glancing at the empty chair opposite.

"You miss him, don't you?" Patience asked, reaching out and taking Noah's hand.

Caleb had left the farmstead shortly after Patience and Noah's wedding. There had been no further animosity, just a realization that their paths lay along different lines. Caleb had never been truly happy as a farmer, not in Ohio and not in Faith's Creek. He needed to see more of the world to discover who he was so that he could be true to himself. Esther Zook had cried for a week, but so had half a dozen other women, and it was soon realized that Caleb was not suited to the simple life which his uncle and Patience had chosen.

"I just hope he's all right, his last letter was a little vague," Noah said, sighing and shaking his head.

"You can't live his life for him. He needs to make his own way in the world and his own mistakes. He's still young enough not to know what he wants and not to need to, either. I sometimes wonder if we need two rumspringa, one to see and one to make sure," Patience replied, as she cleared the plates.

After they had sat for a while by the stove, the two of them made their way back outside into the orchard. It was surrounded by a tall hedge so that within its confines it felt as though a whole world existed, a world hidden away and meant only for them. Patience picked up two stray windfalls, tossing one to Noah and biting into hers with a crunch. It was tart and tangy, refreshing and juicy, and she smiled at the taste of it.

"The best apples in all of Faith's Creek," Noah said, as he climbed up his ladder with a pair of wood shears.

"We're going to have quite a crop to sell at market,"

Patience said, looking around at all the empty trees, now neatly cut back.

It had been an astonishing transformation, the overgrown orchard was now neat and ordered, every tree tended and accounted for. She was proud of Noah's hard work and diligence in bringing it back to life and providing for their future together.

"Not if I fall off this ladder, we won't, hold it steady there, Patience," he said.

She looked up at him and laughed. "I'll catch you if you fall," she said.

He smiled down at her. "I know you would," he said.

When he had finished cutting the branches, he climbed down and looked back up with an air of satisfaction.

"How many more to go?" Patience asked.

Glancing around, he counted. "Five more, and we need to cut back those new fruit bushes at the end. It'll be next year before we see anything from them, but it'll be worth it," he said, "I only wish that Caleb could be here to see it."

"I'm sure he'll come back and see us, but it's high time you focused on what you want, Noah. You've spent so long thinking about others, it's only right that you enjoy the fruits of your labor. I'd say this calls for a celebration," Patience said.

Noah smiled, nodding, and taking her in his arms. "You always know just what to say," he said twirling her around in his arms.

Patience laughed. "The first time you met me, you thought I was all clumsy, and the second time wasn't much better, either," she said, looking up at him and smiling.

"Clumsy with jars and crockery, not with words and sentiments," he replied.

"But I was clumsy with dreams, thinking I knew better than others what was best for me, when all the time I was really waiting for someone else to show me," she said.

"You weren't as clumsy as you thought, and I'm glad about that. All I want is for you to be happy," he said.

"Then you've got your wish," she said, slipping her hand into his, as he kissed her.

"After Eve died, I wondered if I could ever be happy again. You showed me I can be, and that's worth more than anything. I don't want anything but this," he said, casting his hand around the orchard, before gently brushing a finger down her cheek, and kissing her once again.

"I don't ever want to replace her memory, but no one can live in the past, and I'm certain she'd have wanted you to be happy again," Patience said, squeezing his hand.

"She would, and I am – with you," he said, as he held her close.

Patience relaxed into his embrace, knowing that at last her dreams had come true, the unexpected but entirely welcome answer to her prayers.

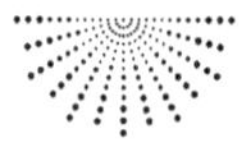

Annie was tidying the schoolhouse. It had been a long but happy day, the children had learned the geography of the states, multiplying by seven, and needlework. She had just rubbed the last remnants of the final lesson from the chalkboard, beating out the duster from the open window, before shutting it and neatening up the desks. She loved this time of day, just as the children had left for home. She liked to imagine them brimming with knowledge, the excitement of a day of learning still hanging in the air.

Neatly, Annie wrote up the next morning's lesson. It was to be spelling and they would be learning several difficult words. She stood back and admired her handiwork, before arranging a pile of textbooks neatly on the side. The exercise books had been collected in and one of the children had left an apple on her desk. She picked it up and took a bite, the sun's rays were streaming in through the window and catching the chalk dust settling in the air.

With a final glance around, Annie put on her shawl and made ready to go home. She would call at Katy Zook's house on the way home to see if the baker had any cinnamon buns left, for they were here *mamm's* favorites. She pulled the blinds down, gave a final glance around the schoolhouse, and stepped out into the afternoon sunshine. Fall had well and truly fallen over Faith's Creek, the path to the lane was covered in brightly colored leaves, which gave Annie an idea for an art project. She was always thinking of new ways to teach the children and see them learn.

Having locked the door to the schoolhouse and waved to Sarah Beiler, who had just passed by with a basket of vegetables in hand, Annie set off along the lane toward her parent's house. She was making a list of all the things she had to do, counting them off one by one and smiling to herself at the thought of what the next day might bring. The children were such characters, and each was growing into their own personality. The auction had raised enough funds to buy many useful things for the schoolhouse and Annie knew she was right where *Gott* intended her to be.

Katy Zook's house lay on the lane just down from that of her parents, and she could smell the scent of cinnamon and sugar in the air as she rounded the corner. Katy had just arrived home from the market and she waved to Annie, beckoning her to follow her inside. The kitchen was warm and the table piled high with all manner of good things to eat. Annie loved the bakery, for she had always enjoyed watching her *mamm* bake cakes and pies at home, though Katy was known to make the best cinnamon buns in the county.

"I'll take six because if Eliza and Patience get wind of them they and their husbands won't waste a moment before coming around," she said, laughing, as Katy bagged up the sweet treats.

"Matthew can smell my cinnamon buns a mile off. He told me as much," Katy said, as Annie handed over her money.

She smiled at the thought of her brother-in-law, he was a good man, and she was so glad that her sister had settled down. So to, Patience, whose new husband was quite the talk of the community. There had been some eyebrows raised when it was discovered that Patience Graber was marrying a man a little older than her. Normally it wouldn't have mattered but Patience had always been so innocent. Many of the community were protective over her, even though she didn't realize it. The muttering continued until Bishop Beiler had pointed out that Abraham and many of the Patriarchs were far older than their wives and as such the matter could be laid to rest. Patience was happy therefore Annie was happy, too.

"Well, good evening, Katy. I'm sure I'll see you soon," Annie said, bidding the baker goodbye.

"Oh, by the way, my cousin Esther is stepping out with Marlin Esch. They make such a delightful pair, they really do," Katy said.

Annie smiled. "I'm glad to hear it," she said and wished the baker good evening again.

It was dusk now, the shadows long in the fields and

hedges, the last of the sun setting on the horizon. Annie was tired, and she was looking forward to finding out what her *mamm* had made for dinner. Perhaps it would be schnitzel, or here favorite butternut pie, the garden had produced a glut of vegetables this year, so much so that her *daed* had been unable to sell them all at the market.

She had just reached the crossroads, where the road led either to Eliza's house or left to her own. She thought about calling in on her sister to deliver Matthew a cinnamon bun, but they would keep until tomorrow and her *daed* did not like her walking home alone in the dark, despite Faith's Creek being surely the safest place in all the United States. She turned left and walked briskly toward home. As she was walking, a noise in the undergrowth to her left startled her and she jumped, stepping back and letting out a cry as a large black shape leaped toward her.

"Oh, how silly," she exclaimed, as Miss Wagler's large black tomcat Arnold wound his way around her legs, "were you looking for mice in there?"

The cat purred.

She fondled its neck for a while, the cat arching its back and rubbing its face further into her hand. It was almost dark now, and Annie petted the cat one last time before shooing him off toward home.

"Don't forget to check the barns," she called after him, smiling to herself, as she walked on.

But now, in the gloom of the lane, the moon had gone behind a cloud, Annie could hear footsteps. She was not sure which direction they came from, for it was rare to meet anyone walking at this time of the evening. The lane only led to her parent's house and she knew that her *mamm* and *daed* would be sat by the stove at this time, not wandering the lane in search of her, for she was often late back from the schoolhouse.

She slowed her pace, and the footsteps seemed to slow, too, the night was now still, save for an owl hooting somewhere in the distance. Annie paused, and the sound paused with her. Her heart was beating fast, and she glanced around her into the gloom but could see nothing. She wondered if she should cry out for help, but would anyone hear her? Or was she just being foolish and imagining things in the dark that were not there?

Overcome with fear, she picked up her pace, fleeing along the lane, longing for the sight of the oil lamp on the porch which showed she was nearly home. But as she ran, she could hear her pursuer behind and she let out a cry, her foot catching in a root snaking out across the path. She went sprawling to the ground, her knees smarting as they scraped in the dirt. She hitched up her skirts and scrambled to her feet, but as she did so, it was not footsteps she heard behind her but a groan, as though someone was injured.

"Help me," a voice stuttered in the darkness.

Annie peered cautiously through the gloom. "Hello? Whos' there?" she called out, but there only came further groaning. Summoning her courage, and keeping all her wits about her, Annie stepped back along the trail.

She had always been a brave woman, one who stood no nonsense from anyone, and now she intended to discover who it was that had followed her. It was not far back along the lane that she found the source of the groans, but it came as a shock for her to discover who it was that lay there. It was Caleb, his face all bruised and bloody. Annie reached down to help him, shaking her head in astonishment.

"Caleb? I thought you'd left Faith's Creek behind? What are you doing here? What happened to you?" she asked, unsure if it was Caleb who had been following her or someone in whose way Caleb had found himself.

"Help me, Annie, please," he gasped.

Annie nodded. "Don't you worry, let's get you... oh, maybe not," she said to herself, imagining that her parents may not be too pleased to see a bloodied Caleb King on their doorstep that evening.

"Please, Annie, I need help," he gasped.

Annie helped him to his feet. She was used to dealing with bumps and bruises, with all the scrapes and scratches which the children brought in from play at the schoolhouse and she knew that back there she had a first aid kit with the necessary items to clean and tend to his wounds.

"What happened to you?" she asked, but Caleb could only groan, and repeat his call for help.

"All right, don't you worry, I'll help you," she said, determinedly, taking him under the arm and helping him back toward the schoolhouse...

In case you missed it read on for a preview of Eliza's Faith

"Do you think he'll be there?" Eliza Graber asked as she and her two sisters sat around the kitchen table.

It had been raining that afternoon and the Graber sisters, Annie, the eldest, Eliza, and their younger sister Patience, were busy with their needlework. Their mother, Barbara, took a batch of freshly baked rolls from the oven, filling the house with the scent of baking. She looked up and smiled, shaking her head.

"It hardly matters if he is or isn't, you'll never pluck up the courage to speak to him," Annie said, laying down her needlework, as Patience giggled.

"I will," Eliza replied, hurt by her sister's lack of confidence in her.

"You could have spoken to him at the picnic last week." Annie raised her eyebrows.

"Or after the service last month. He was all on his own, just sitting alone," Patience continued.

Eliza sighed. Her sisters were right, of course, and she wondered whether she would ever have the courage to speak with Matthew Lloyd, their friend and neighbor, who also happened to be the man she was in love with. He had blossomed from a gangly boy into a strapping and handsome man, with dark blond hair and beautiful blue eyes. She was not the only woman in Faith's Creek who had fallen for him, and she had her doubts as to his feelings for her. Still, she could dream, though as Annie so often pointed out, a dream is nothing if you do not move towards it... if it had no hope of coming true.

"I'm sure your sister knows what she's doing," Barbara said, placing the rolls onto the cooling rack and dusting off her apron.

"She's going to be left on the shelf if she's not careful," Annie said, and Eliza laughed.

"You're the eldest, I don't see any signs of you finding

a husband," she said, and Annie gave her a withering look.

"You know I don't intend to marry, I want to be a schoolteacher and I can't do that if I'm chasing after husbands now, can I?" she said.

Eliza smiled. She had always liked teasing her elder sister, who, in truth, could wed any man she wished. She was beautiful, with dark brown hair and hazel eyes, a soft complexion, and rosy cheeks, and Eliza knew that any number of young men in Faith's Creek would be happy to make their proposal to her.

"Oh, do speak to him, Eliza, you must. Tonight's the perfect opportunity," Patience said, putting her hand on Eliza's and smiling.

"You're such a romantic, Patience. You think that just because I speak to Matthew, there'll be a wedding next week," Eliza replied, and her younger sister laughed.

"I just want you to be happy, is that so awful? He's perfect for you, The two of you have been friends for so long, wouldn't it just be wonderful if you got married," Patience said, appearing misty-eyed, as though caught up in her own fantasy.

"It has its attractions," Eliza admitted, glancing at the clock on the kitchen wall.

"We'd better get ready, you know what they're like, board games wait for no man, or woman," Annie said.

The three sisters rose to their feet. They were to attend a board games evening at a local farm, where there was a barn big enough for all the town's young people to come together. It was organized by Bishop Amos Beiler and the three sisters had been looking forward to it ever since the announcement had been made at service last month.

"Go and wash your faces and get ready," their *mamm* said, smiling at the three of them, as Patience and Annie clattered up the stairs from the kitchen.

"Should I speak with him *Mamm*?" Eliza asked, and her mother smiled.

"You should do what you think is right, Eliza. Matthew Lloyd is a good man, His parents have always been good friends and neighbors to us and I'm sure he'd make a good husband for you, though I don't always agree with women making the first move. You might wait and see what he has to say for himself first."

Eliza nodded. "I'll try not to get too caught up in the idea," she said, but her *mamm* shook her head.

"There's no harm in dreaming, Eliza. Hurry now, or you'll be late," Barbara said.

With a smile, Eliza made her way upstairs.

Patience had just finished in the bathroom and now Eliza splashed water on her face and lathered up the soap, gazing at herself for a moment in the mirror. She had always thought her elder sister to be the prettiest woman she knew, though Patience, with her blonde hair and blue eyes, was fast blossoming too. Eliza was something of them both, with light brown hair and similarly colored eyes. She washed the soap from her face and dried it with a rough towel, before putting on her kapp and joining her sisters on the landing.

"Ready?" Annie asked, and Eliza nodded.

They made their way back downstairs, where their *daed*, Samuel, had just come in from feeding the chickens in the yard. The girls lived with their parents on a small homestead on the edge of town, the family's home for three generations. It was a happy life and one which Eliza had come to cherish, even if her Rumspringa had shown her more of the world than she might have imagined.

"Look at you three, aren't you a picture," Samuel said, and all three girls smiled.

"Are you walking them over to Jackson's farm?" Barbara asked, and their *daed* nodded.

"It's a nice evening, I might even call on Bishop Beiler on my way back," he said.

"You three enjoy yourselves, now," Barbara said, kissing each of them on the cheek.

"We will," Patience replied.

"And remember what I said," Barbara said, turning to Eliza, who blushed.

"What did Mamm say to you?" Annie asked as soon as they were outside.

"Now then, I don't want any tittle-tattle," Samuel said, as Patience took him by the arm.

"Eliza's going to speak with Matthew Lloyd tonight," she said, and their *daed* raised an eyebrow.

"Is that so?" he asked, causing Eliza to blush.

She hated to think that her *daed* might be displeased with her. She cared about what he thought and so far, she had kept the subject of marriage a close secret, confiding in no one but her *mamm* as to her true feelings, though they were plain to see.

"I like him," she admitted.

"He's a *gut* man, he comes from a *gut* family. I wouldn't stand against it, though I'd have preferred it if you'd asked me first. I've never been strict with you girls, but when it comes to my daughters, I like to know what's going on," he said, giving Eliza a firm look.

"He probably won't even be there and if he is, I doubt he'll feel the same. He'll say we're just friends or something like that," Eliza sighed, wishing she had never even mentioned it.

Her feelings for Matthew were clear, but what was also clear was that a dozen other women in Faith's

Creek would happily have that same conversation with him. She might be in love with him, but that was no reason for him to be in love with her. With her nerves rising, Eliza lagged behind the others, her heart beating fast at the prospect of what was to come.

"It's good of you to walk us *Daed*," Annie said, as they came to the track leading up to Jackson's farm, where the game night was to take place in one of the barns.

"Nonsense, I'm happy to, and I'll come to walk you home later on," he said, smiling, as he kissed all three of them goodbye.

"Give our regards to Bishop Beiler," Annie called out, and their father waved his hand.

"Enjoy yourselves," he said, as the three sisters walked arm in arm up the track toward the farm.

Eliza wondered if she should go home, surely this was going to be a disaster?

The sun was beginning to set and the barn was lit by lamps, making the place look homey and welcoming.

Already a dozen or so of their friends and acquaintances had gathered. Haybales had been positioned around the barn, with chess sets and draught boards laid out on each, and at the far end was a low trestle table, covered in all manner of good things to eat.

"Doesn't it look lovely," Patience said, waving to several of her friends, who came hurrying over.

"I'm sure I'm getting too old for this, if I keep coming to these things I'll soon be teaching half of them," Annie said, as she and Eliza watched Patience be made a fuss of by her friends.

"You enjoy it really, I know you do," Eliza said, turning to her sister, who raised her eyebrows.

"Well, I enjoy beating you all at chess, though I shouldn't be so proud," she said with a wink.

Eliza laughed. "You've got a talent, use it, don't hide your lamp under a bushel, that's what the Bible says," Eliza said, and now it was Annie's turn to laugh.

"It also says a lot about vanity and pride. Anyway, have you seen him yet?" she asked, glancing around.

Eliza looked too, though she could see no sign of Matthew, nor any of the young men he hung out with. She was just about to sit down at one of the haybales and challenge Annie to a game of draughts when voices along the track caused her to turn. She knew Matthew's voice, even without seeing him, and he was calling out a greeting to Mr. Jackson's son, Marlin.

With a smile, she turned, ready to greet him, but the smile soon fell from her face and she let out an anguished gasp. There was Matthew, entering the barn, a smile on his face, but on his arm, was Betty Lapp, the sight of which brought a tear to her eye. She clutched at Annie, who sighed and shook her head, as Betty waved to them, a look of pride on her face. Betty Lapp was a stunning beauty, one who could have her choice of any man she wished and by the looks of it, she had chosen Matthew ...

Read Eliza's Faith now on Amazon

ALSO BY SARAH MILLER

All my books are FREE on Kindle Unlimited

If you love Amish Romance, the sweet, clean stories of Sarah Miller you can join me for the latest news on upcoming books http://eepurl.com/bdEdSn

These are some of my reader favorites:

Amish Spring Baby

A Love Tested

Find all Sarah's books on Amazon and click the yellow follow button

This book is dedicated to the wonderful Amish people and the faithful life that they live.

Go in peace my friends.

As an independent author, Sarah relies on your support. If you enjoyed this book, please leave a review on Amazon or Goodreads.

ABOUT THE AUTHOR

Sarah Miller was born in Pennsylvania and spent her childhood close to the Amish people. Weekends were spent doing chores; quilting or eventually babysitting in the community. She grew up to love their culture and the simple lifestyle and had many Amish friends. The one thing that you can guarantee when you are near the Amish, Sarah believes is that you will feel close to God.

Many years later she married Martin who is the love of her life and moved to England. There she started to write stories about the Amish. Recently after a lot of persuasion from her best friend she has decided to publish her stories. They draw on inspiration from her relationship with the Amish and with God and she hopes you enjoy reading them as much as she did writing them. Many of the stories are based on true events but names have been changed and even though they are authentic at times artistic license has been used.

Sarah likes her stories simple and to hold a message and they help bring her closer to her faith. She currently lives in Yorkshire, England with her husband Martin and seven very spoiled chickens.

She would love to meet you on Facebook at https://www.facebook.com/SarahMillerBooks

Sarah hopes her stories will both entertain and inspire and she wishes that you go with God.